THE PEN PIEYU ADVENTURES

SIR PRINCESS PETRA'S TALENT

Seek your Talents!

The Pen Pieyu Adventures

Sir Princess Petra's Talent

Book Two

Diane Mae Robinson

TATE PUBLISHING
AND ENTERPRISES, LLC

Published by Tate Publishing & Enterprises, LLC
127 E. Trade Center Terrace | Mustang, Oklahoma 73064 USA
1.888.361.9473 | www.tatepublishing.com

Tate Publishing is committed to excellence in the publishing industry. The company reflects the philosophy established by the founders, based on Psalm 68:11,
"The Lord gave the word and great was the company of those who published it."

Book design copyright © 2013 by Tate Publishing, LLC. All rights reserved.
Cover and Interior design by Errol Villamante
Illustrations by Samantha Kickingbird

Published in the United States of America

ISBN: 978-1-62510-682-7
1. Juvenile Fiction / Fantasy & Magic
2. Juvenile Fiction / Action & Adventure / General
15.11.10

DEDICATION

For Allen.

ACKNOWLEDGMENT

It takes a whole kingdom to raise a child.

Praise for *Sir Princess Petra: The Pen Pieyu Adventures, Book 1*

"Her writing grabs you, is perfectly pitched, nuanced, a fresh approach."
—Lieutenant Governor of Alberta
Emerging Artist Award adjudicators

Sir Princess Petra: The Pen Pieyu Adventures is a maverick fantasy, packed with plot twists and turns, unexpected obstacles and problems, and brilliant flashes of humor and originality. *Sir Princess Petra* charms and entrances the reader.
—James A. Cox,
The Midwest Book Review

Sir Princess Petra is a delightfully imaginative storytime read and reread. Petra's character is both confident and charismatic. Further, Robinson's empowering story is accompanied by beautifully shaded pencil drawings that illustrate Petra's royal quest. I highly recommend *Sir Princess Petra* for school, public, and personal library collections.
—Natalie Schembri,
University of Manitoba Reviews

This is a great book for elementary schools and public libraries. I would highly recommend this.

—Brenda Ballard for Readers Favorite

Sir Princess Petra is one of those stories that will appeal to most everybody. It is charmingly funny. The author's imagination is appropriately childlike. I know Petra is a child every parent will love.

—Sue Morris, Kid Lit Reviews

Ms. Robinson had created an interesting and delightful tale about acceptance and understanding. Her characters are fun, and children will enjoy the spunkiness of Petra. Children seven and up will love this unique chapter book.

—Renee Hand,
The Crypto-Capers Review

This book has a great story line and a great message about believing in yourself. Petra proves that she and all girls can be daring, adventurous, and brave. This is an awesome chapter book.

—Erik, This Kid Reviews Books

Diane Mae Robinson delivers a very interesting and spell-binding book in "Sir Princess Petra. This is a book of courage for every young boy or girl to not give up on their dreams and press on unhindered."

—Darin Godby for Readers Favorite

Sir Princess Petra – The Pen Pieyu Adventures is a tale of adventure and humor with a charismatic main character who has a lot of heart. Certainly a book that children will enjoy again and again.

—Stacie Theis, Book Reviewer, Beachboundbooks

Sometimes a kids book comes along that turns convention on its ear. This is one such book. The book also has messages of kindness and understanding winning out over brute force and fighting.

—John L. Hoh Jr., Book Ideas.com

MAP OF
PEN PIEYU KINGDOM
AND SURROUNDING LANDS

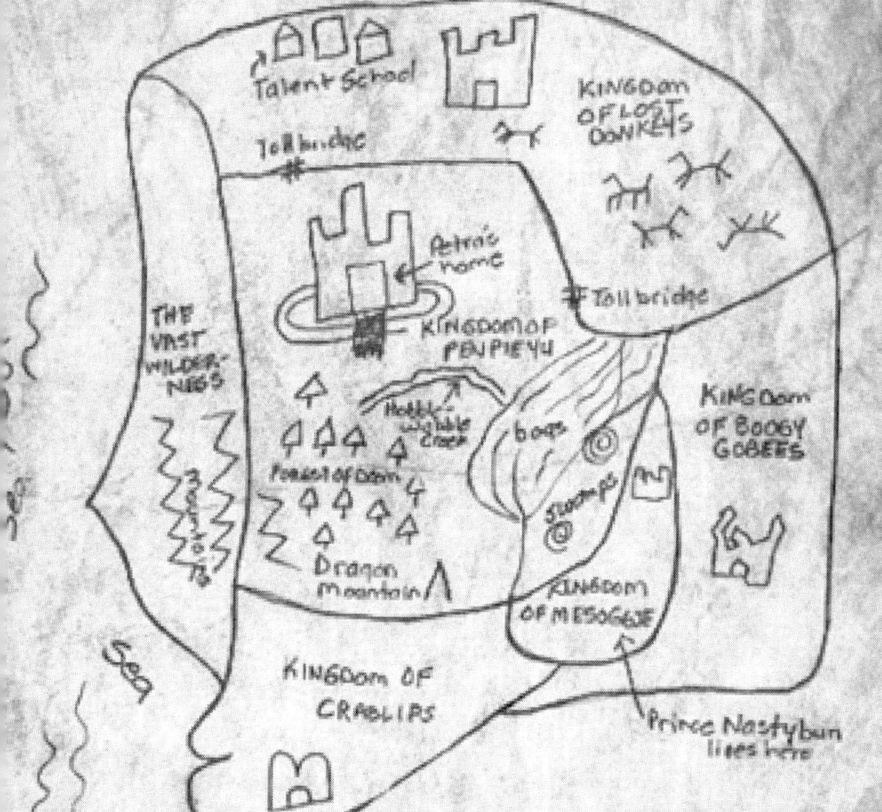
Talent School
KINGDOM OF LOST DONKEYS
Tollbridge
Petra's home
Tollbridge
THE VAST WILDERNESS
KINGDOM OF BOOGY GOBEES
bogs
Swamps
Forest of Doom
Dragon mountain
Sea
KINGDOM OF CRABLIPS
Prince Nastybun lives here
swamps
bogs
mountains
Forest
Sea

D.M. Robinson

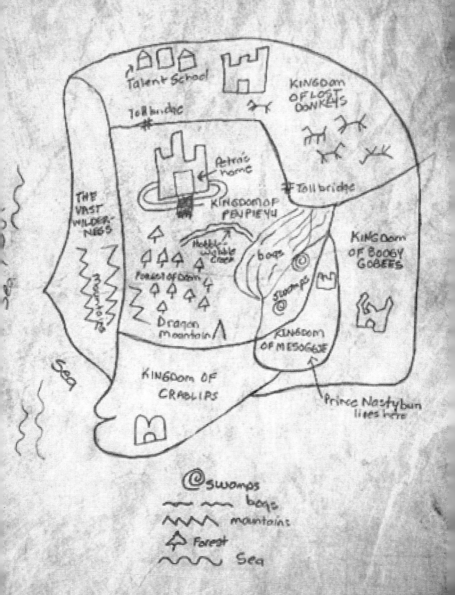

SYNOPSIS OF
BOOK ONE

At Longstride Castle, in the Kingdom of Pen Pieyu, it is Princess Petra's ninth and royal birthday. Her father, King Longstride, has promised her anything her heart desires. Petra chooses to become a royal knight and protect her kingdom. (Thus far, Longstride castle has no knights as all of the silly soldiers are still trying to become knights.)

After much commotion in the royal throne room, King Longstride has no choice but to grant her request. The royal rule book says nothing about a girl becoming a knight but only that the proposed knight must perform a deed from a list of three. The choices are: to capture a crocodile and make his skin into a royal leather chair; to hush the howling, nasty dragon, Snarls, in the Forest of Doom; or to eat a roomful of raw onions.

Petra chooses to hush the howling, nasty dragon, Snarls. Outfitted in the best royal pots and pans, Petra heads off into the Forest of Doom with nothing more than her cake knife sword and a sack of onions to search out the dragon.

After a few strange encounters in the Forest of Doom, Petra finally confronts Snarls; and after some onion-throwing and eyebrow-singeing, she discovers not all is as it seems. Snarls is howling because his tail is stuck under a pile of fallen rocks, not because he is mean and nasty. Petra helps Snarls escape his predicament, and the two become fast friends.

Petra returns to the castle to announce her accomplishment of hushing the howling dragon and, thus, gains her real armour. Thereafter, she is forever known as Sir Princess Petra.

Of course, Petra and Snarls go on to have more adventures and encounter other zany characters: Bograt, the bog witch; Prince Nastybun and his midget army; and Letgo, the crocodile.

And Pen Pieyu Kingdom has never been the same.

INTRODUCTION

Over the last several months, Longstride Castle had become quite accustomed to having the only Princess Knight, well, the only knight actually, in the lands of Pen Pieyu. The king and queen held many parties in Petra's honor, and royals and peasants alike acknowledged the Princess Knight's kindness and bravery and brought what gifts they could to the castle, although the gift bearing seemed to have slowed of late.

Petra was not concerned with the parties or gifts as much as she was eager to practice all her knight skills: jousting, fencing, javelin throwing, steed grooming and maintenance, running, armour polishing, and, of course, onion-throwing to hit the mark. She also kept up with her Highland dance lessons, just because she liked it.

Longstride Castle had also become quite accustomed to having a dragon in the kitchen since Snarls had become master barbecue connoisseur. The royal rule book said nothing about a dragon in the kitchen, only that the master barbecue connoisseur must provide a very hot fire available for barbecues at a moment's notice. The castle parties flourished as Snarls roasted to perfection his specialities: skewed onion-turnip pom-poms, onion-broccoli no-where-to-be-seen, and, of course, onion omelette ta-da.

CHAPTER 1

THE ROYAL RULE BOOK, AGAIN

Petra awoke to the sound of the royal councilman's bugle. She hastily dressed in leggings and a tunic full of rips and holes from a recent jousting practice and scurried to the royal throne room.

The king and queen of Pen Pieyu sat upon their ragged, leather thrones. Her mother had a nervous look about her, and her father, a sly grin. The royal councilman was running in circles until he came upon the royal rule book, which lay under Claymore, the royal mastiff. Somehow, Petra thought, the royal rule book looked much thicker than last she had seen it. That could only mean trouble. Petra rolled her eyes and gave a little moan.

"Father, Mother," Petra said with a bow, "you summoned me?"

"Yes, my little Princess Knight," her father replied, rather surly, as he watched the royal councilman point to a section in the royal rule book. The king stood, cleared his throat, then bellowed out, "It is hereby written that all Princess Knights of the Kingdom of Pen Pieyu must attend Talent School before their tenth year of age. They will be sent to the Land of Lost Donkeys and, under the instruction and guidance of King Asterman, learn a talent fit for a princess. After which time, the hereby-said princess—meaning you—will return to the Kingdom of Pen Pieyu with a proper princess talent and a certificate."

Petra felt her face flush and her manners fly out the window. "That is ridiculous! I am a royal knight since I have accomplished the deed of hushing the howling dragon, Snarls, in the Forest of Doom. I should be treated as a royal knight and not this sissy princess stuff! And, besides, you just wrote that part—"

"Silence!" the king roared.

The royal councilman's eyes grew extremely wide. He flipped the page of the royal book and backed away.

The king gave his you-had-better-be-quiet glare toward Petra, then continued to read, loudly, "The hereby-said Princess Knight will acquire a talent certificate or be in forfeit of this royal rule. Forfeiting this royal rule will entitle the royal magician to turn the hereby-said Princess Knight into a frog to live in the bogs for a period of five years." The king smirked and plopped back onto his chair.

"You made that all up!" Petra gave her best that's-not-fair stare. "Our kingdom has never had a Princess Knight, nor any knight for that matter, before me. And as if a person can be turned into a frog." She wondered about this for just a moment. "At any rate, I would rather be a frog than learn to crochet!" Petra blurted and crossed her arms.

The queen's face paled; then, her head swirled in three full circles before flopping over unto the side wing of her chair. The king, again, stood up, but this time, he seemed much taller than before. He snapped his fingers, and promptly, the royal magician appeared. The royal magician had strange, purple sparks spitting out all around him, and his long, white hair was standing straight up in wiggling, twisted ropes. Nine frogs, draped in nine much-too-large soldier tunics, hopped around before disappearing under the magician's robes.

This was all quite shocking to Petra, especially since she didn't know they even had a royal magician. She immediately peeked into the royal onion room. The nine palace soldiers were not there. They were always there, trying to accomplish one of the royal rule book deeds by eating a roomful of raw onions and, hence, winning their knight status. Only Bograt, the bog witch, was in the onion room, humming and munching away. Petra felt a lump in her

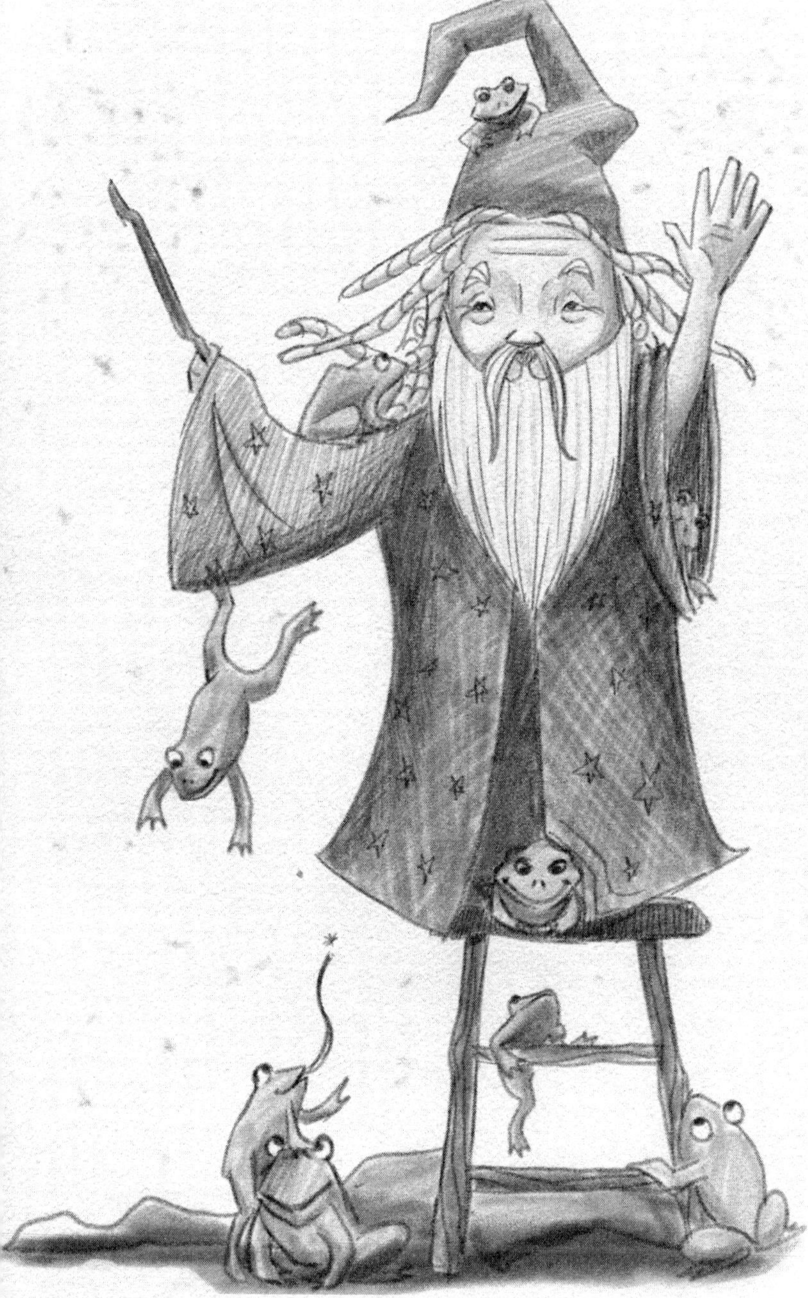

throat and swallowed hard. "All right, Father. I will go. But I insist to bring Snarls, since he is my royal dragon steed, and I insist to wear my knight armour."

"Fine. That will be fine," the king said, waving her off. He whispered out of the side of his mouth to the queen, "She's going, my dear. We have won this nonsense knight issue of hers once and for all."

"But what of the royal barbecues if she takes Snarls?" the queen muttered back, her head still in the flopped-over position.

Petra turned on her heels and stomped off to the armoury. "Urrrr. They can't turn me into a girly princess just because it's in that silly rule book. I am not learning any useless knitting, or whatever, stuff—and that's that!"

The armoury guard had readied the armour and offered her the breastplate first.

"Just my chain mail and helmet will be fine. Oh, and my sack of onions, of course." She smiled at the old guard. "A knight always needs onions."

He fetched everything immediately. There was a new pink plume on her helmet since Snarls had accidently scorched the last one. This plume was much bigger and incredibly better than the last one, but the weight of it tended to make her helmet tilt forward. She had an idea. Grabbing up the long twines that held the onion sack closed, she strung a twine through each of the ear loops of the helmet and tied a knot. This seemed to level the helmet perfectly.

"Snarls, you look fantastic," Petra gushed when the dragon shuffled in.

"Um, this saddle is pink." Snarls' cheeks seemed to reflect the same pinkish hue of the saddle as he twisted this way and that, trying to get a better look. "And what's with these tassels?"

Petra giggled. "You look as a dashing steed should," she said and mounted the stirrup on his left. "Giddy-up, Snarls, off to the Land of Lost Donkeys."

CHAPTER 2

PRINCE DUCE CRABLIPS

As the pair moseyed north toward the Land of Lost Donkeys, Petra and Snarls reminisced about some of the great barbecue parties the castle had held lately.

"Actually, it's kind of nice to get out of the kitchen," Snarls remarked. "I think when we get back, I'll have to talk with the king about vacation time."

"You deserve it, Snarls. Since you've become master barbecuer, Mother has had everybody and their royal mule over for a party several times over. Hey, Prince Nastybun and the knights of Mesoggie should be back soon for their usual drying-off visit. After your vacation, let's throw them another humdinger party. That will be fun."

"Yah, if the magician doesn't turn them into frogs first," Snarls said, then added with a chuckle, "Nothing worse than the smell of soggy frogs I say."

They both burst out laughing.

Their laughter was abruptly halted when they noticed the strange knight standing sentry at the foot of the toll bridge. He had on armour in different hues of pink. The breastplate was painted with a bouquet of wild flowers, and his helmet was a weird oblong shape that outlined his weird oblong face. His lips were unusually huge and reminded Petra of a camel. He stood with his feet apart and held his pink spear horizontally across his chest.

"Should I say 'yikes' now?" Snarls whispered to Petra.

Everybody just blinked at each other for some time before Petra asked, "Is there something you want?"

The pink knight spoke with a vibrating voice, "I am Prince Duce Crablips of the Kingdom of Crablips. I aim to stop the Princess Knight from acquiring a talent and gaining her certificate. I will stop at nothing. We may have to duel if you do not turn back."

"What in the entire kingdom are you talking about?" Petra frowned her eyebrows at him.

"Are you not the Princess Knight?"

"Yes, I am Petra Longstride of the Kingdom of Pen Pieyu."

"Oh no, not another do-well?" Snarls grumbled. "The last time you had a do-well, you squeezed and squished and twirled Prince Nastybun in your dance routine for so long…well, he did finally give up, but honestly, it was just boring. Don't you know of any other do-well maneuvers?"

"It's a duel, Snarls, not a do-well."

"I know all about your little clutch-'em-dance routine," Duce Crablips blurted. "And you're not touching me!"

"I have no intentions of touching you or dueling with you." Petra said, feeling quite sure she was becoming annoyed. "But why in the kingdom would you care if I received my talent certificate?"

Duce Crablips dropped to one knee, shouldered his spear to point at them, and began chanting something that sounded in between humming in Chinese and the rusty wheels of the royal wheat mill.

"Stop that! I can't understand a word you're saying, and it's all quite harmful to the ear!" Petra slid down the smooth scales of her mount.

Duce Crablips let loose his spear.

It landed between Snarls' toes.

Snarls yanked the spear from the dirt, broke it in two, then, raised his head and blew out a fierce stream of something that resembled torn pieces of gooey parchment.

"Oops." Snarls flashed a fake smile. "Possibly too many onions in that last omelette ta-da?"

"Snarls, stop dragon blasting!" Petra snapped. "And as for you, Duce Crablips, just tell me what your problem is, and you won't be reported for interfering with my mission!"

Duce, covered in layers of sticky onion skins, looked like something ready to bake. His eyes, as wide as royal platters, were wider than his wide lips. He slowly stood up on shaking legs.

"Is it true they put you in a frilly dress for interfering with someone's mission?" he whimpered.

"Worse for messing with a knight!" Petra scolded. "It's a strict rule in my kingdom."

"Oh, now what should I do, dear me, what, what, what?" Duce Crablips contorted his face to go from confusion, to worry, to outright fright. "I just don't want to be engaged to you!" he cried.

Snarls snickered and squinted his eyes. "Why, my little Princess Knight, have you been keeping your true royal age a secret?"

Petra glared back and forth at both of them. "I am nine and one quarter. And no, I'm not engaging pink knight or anybody for that matter. And what does a talent certificate have to do with getting engaged?" she demanded of Duce.

Prince Duce Crablips sniffled and blew a loud honk into his pink hankie. "Oh, thank the crab gods, you don't agree to the engaging," he said. "But whatever shall we do? My father sent a scroll to your father many new moons ago saying, just a minute, I have a scribe's copy here somewhere." He patted around his armour and finally plucked out a scroll from under his armpit, unrolled it, and read:

"I, King Crablips, of the Kingdom of Crablips, decree and agree with myself that when King Longstride, of the Kingdom of Pen Pieyu, acquires a Princess Knight with a talent certificate, then the hereby-said Princess Knight and Prince Duce Crablips will become immediately engaged, thus binding them to marriage at the proper royal age, and henceforth the immediate engagement uniting our kingdoms to have immediate access to more soldiers whereupon the enhanced, unified army will procure the final defeat of that nasty Prince Nastybun and his puny army from the Kingdom of Mesoggie."

"Well, I'm sure glad we got that out of the way," Petra chuckled. "How long have you been waiting here? The knights of Mesoggie have befriended the Kingdom of Pen Pieyu at least three new moons ago. There is no need for a ridiculous engagement."

"Really? Truly? You wouldn't jest me?" Duce's grin spread fast and wide. "Oh, what a relief. Thank the crab gods again and again and again."

"This is all just a silly mix up," Petra assured him. "I'll talk to my father. I'm sure the Kingdom of Crablips will be a welcome ally in our lands nonetheless."

Petra wondered at something. "How did you know I'd enter by this toll bridge? There is another toll bridge to the east."

Duce hesitated a moment. "Well, from Bograt."

"You know Bograt?" Petra and Snarls said in unison.

"Oh yes. The bog witch has been a friend of our kingdom for years ever since we made a deal with her. We give her all the beetroots she wants, and she doesn't eat us."

Petra and Snarls looked at each other and burst into a bent-over laughter.

"What's so funny?" Duce asked, looking a little insulted.

"Well, Duce…you've been hoodwinked," Snarls answered, trying to catch his breath. "Bograt…doesn't eat people, only vegetables."

They all had a great laugh as they clutched hands and claws.

"Say, while you're all the way up here, why don't you join us for Talent School?" Petra suggested.

"You know, I've always wanted to learn to crochet," Duce replied.

"Yah, well, you're not getting anywhere near my fancy saddle with that mess all over you," Snarls informed Duce.

"It's okay, Snarls, we'll walk. It's not far now."
Petra led the way.

CHAPTER 3

THE LAND OF LOST DONKEYS

As the trio approached Talent School in the Land of Lost Donkeys, a tall man dressed in a ragged cloak and torn robes was frantically waving his arms as he raced out to greet them. This must be King Asterman, Petra thought as she spied the embroidered name on his cloak that said, "King Asterman". But King Asterman must have been too excited because he ran right past them.

Soon, Petra realized his predicament. His robes had a problem. King Asterman continued running, screeching, and hollering for some time while his flaming robes flew out behind him. Suddenly, he stopped, dropped, and rolled, then instantly sprang up, and marched toward them with his chin tilted high. His robes were still smoking.

"Oh, never mind that. We have it under control," he said, still a little breathless, while indicating the smoldering grass. "Barbecue School isn't going so well."

"Hey, I love barbecues!" Snarls piped up. "I have my repertoire of recipes memorized."

"Why... Um..." King Asterman looked over the three of them. "Who are you?"

"Hello. I'm Petra Longstride of the Kingdom of Pen Pieyu. I think you've been expecting me.

These are my friends, Prince Duce Crablips of the Kingdom of Crablips and Snarls of the Forest of Doom."

"Oh, my… well, certainly. Are you all here for Talent School? I was only expecting the princess."

Snarls and Duce eyed each other and grinned.

"I'd just love to learn crochet and maybe knitting," Duce sang out.

"And I can show you a thing or two about Barbecue School," Snarls boasted as he whipped out a scroll, which unraveled at King Asterman's feet. "Here is my résumé."

"You carry a résumé?" Petra asked, raising her eyebrows.

"Yes, I see. Okay then." King Asterman had a puzzled look on his face. "And you, my dear, what is your desired princess talent?"

Snarls and Duce skedaddled off to their schools of choice, leaving Petra to deal with King Asterman alone.

"I am a knight." Petra straightened her posture. "I already know how to ride my steed well, throw a javelin and hit the mark, joust to upend the biggest of soldiers, and I even know how to tame a crocodile. I certainly don't know what else I could possible learn to benefit my knight skills."

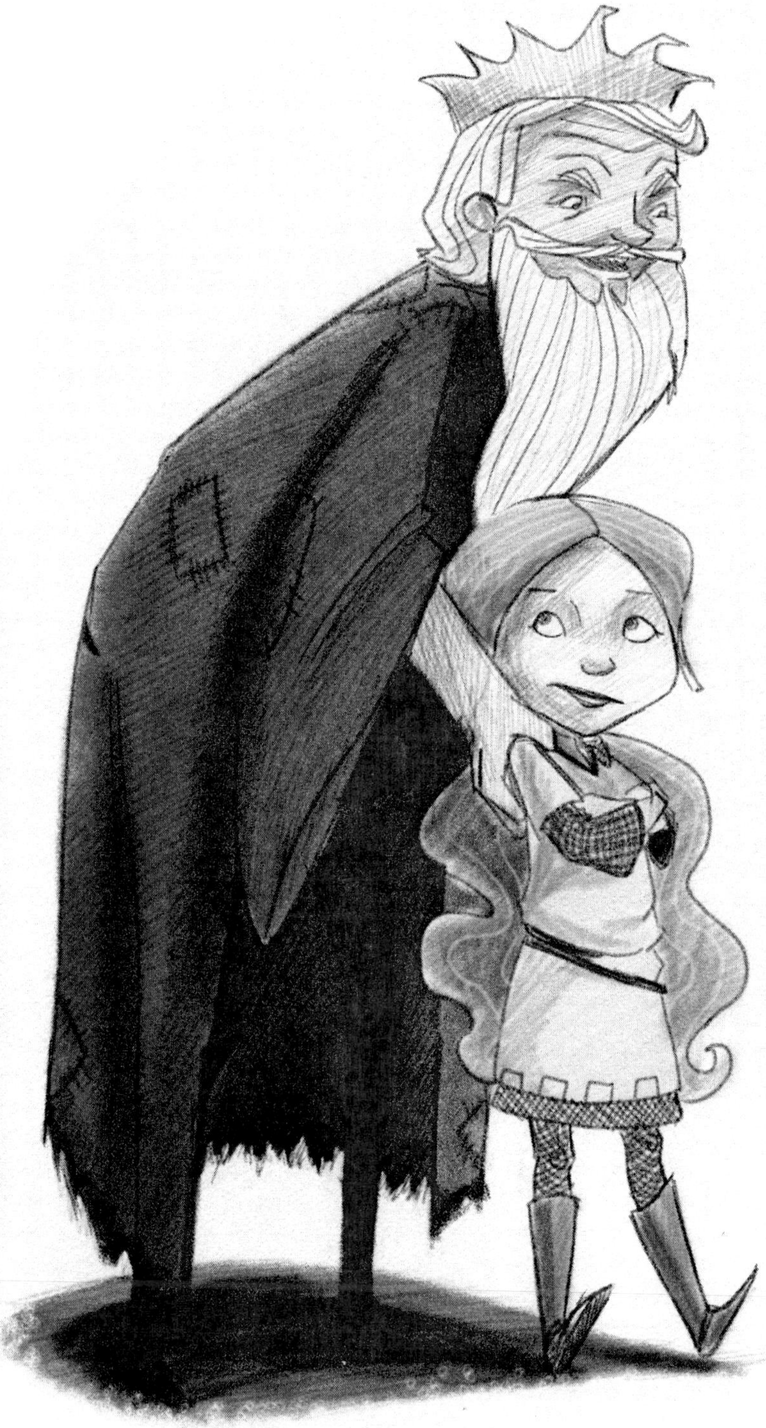

"Yes, yes, your father told me all about your… um… other skills. But now, you must earn a certificate in a princess trade."

Petra frowned her eyebrows as she studied the different buildings and read the following: Princess Etiquette School, Knitting School, Barbecue School, Crochet School, Get Over Fainting Fast School, Jewelry Budgeting School, Cloak Sewing School, Preparing To Be Engaged School.

"No, no, no, and definitely not!" Petra huffed. "But what of that? Why does it say 'Ferrier School Closed'? I might like that."

"Oh, that. Now that was a bad idea, very, very bad idea," King Asterman claimed, shaking his head. "Anyway, all the donkeys are gone. There are no animals to practice on."

"I could practice on my trusty steed, Snarls."

King Asterman blinked his eyelashes very fast. "Oh, no, no. That would be impossible. The donkeys took all the tools when they disappeared. Ferrier School is closed indefinitely."

"Hmm, how strange," Petra wondered. "Then I will pick that one, Writing School."

"Actually, that one is closed also." King Asterman stepped in front of her, trying to block her view.

Petra peeked around his big belly. "There is no closed sign."

"What? Oh, it must have fallen off, then. You can't go there." King Asterman turned her in the direction of Knitting School and shooed her along.

Petra stood firm. "No, there is no closed sign. I will attend Writing School."

King Asterman groaned and smacked his forehead. He was muttering something about one day catching up with those troublemaking donkeys.

CHAPTER 4

TALENT SCHOOL

King Asterman stomped toward Writing School, still muttering and mumbling—this time, something about being put in a frilly dress when King Longstride finds out. Petra smiled and followed.

Once inside, Petra positioned herself into the first of the five desks and wondered at the bareness of the walls and the lack of books in the classroom. King Asterman squeezed behind the desk at the front of the class.

"Will nobody else be attending, sir?"

"No. Talent School is in a bit of a lull right now. So to begin Knitting School—"

Petra fired up her hand. "Excuse me. We're in Writing School. That's what I signed up for, remember?"

"Yes, yes, of course." King Asterman huffed out a big breath. "Then open your English book to page twenty-six. We'll begin with formations of noun plurals, proper nouns, correct pronoun use, and then on to subordinate clauses—"

Petra fired up her hand again. "Excuse me, sir, I have no book. And I already know some of that from my home schooling. That's all real boring and mostly for adults."

"What part of writing do you want to learn then?" King Asterman growled.

Petra tapped her quill pen on her cheek and tried to think. It was very distracting with all the whooping and hollering and cheering coming from Barbecue School next door.

"Hmm, well, I like to use my good imagination, so … I know, I'll do poetry," she decided.

Now, King Asterman's eyebrows twitched, and his lips quivered. He seemed very near to having some sort of fit.

"Okay, okay!" His voice became very strict. "Go to your dorm, and read all the chapters on poetry forms and rules. Memorize the forms and write me a poem by morning."

"But I have no book, sir."

King Asterman settled back in his chair, crossed his arms, and grinned.

~~~~~~~~~~

Petra wrote and scribbled throughout the evening and late into the night. Snarls and Duce snored with a loud synchronized rhythm that vibrated her bunk and kept her awake anyway. An idea came to her—their snoring had a beat pattern, like a song—and her good imagination kicked in.

Early the next morning, Petra was already waiting outside the Writing School when King

Asterman arrived. He had on the same winning grin as he had on yesterday. They entered the school and settled into their desks.

"Good morning. Did you find the assignment too difficult perhaps? Are you ready for something easier? Something more fit for a princess, say like crocheting or—"

Petra raised her arm. "The ballad is poetry in song. The sonnet is usually a fourteen-line verse of strict rhyming scheme: abab, cdcd, efef, gg. The limerick is a five-line humorous poem where lines one, two, and five rhyme—"

"Enough!" King Asterman slammed his hand on the desk. He seemed surprised by his own outburst. "How do you know that?"

"Well, I just recall reading it in home school lessons. Am I right?"

King Asterman opened his mouth into a scream shape, but no scream came out.

"All right, I'm getting there." Petra worried at his impatience. "I've written a rhyming poem. I think it follows the rules, but more importantly, I've used my good imagination. And I think it would make a good ballad." Petra unraveled her scroll to land at the edge of King Asterman's desk.

He groaned, grabbed the scroll, and read aloud,

Jimmy Jamsmacker loved to eat jam.
Even preferred it to succulent ham.
It was all that he ate, day in and day out.
What was for supper? He had no doubt.
"Jimmy Jamsmacker," his mother did say,
"You have to eat something different today.
The cupboards are bare, the jam has run out.
Maybe you could go catch a trout."
Jimmy frowned, squinted one eye,
Threw open the cupboards. "It must be a lie!"
Nothing was left, not a lick in a jar.
He would have to go searching no matter how far.
Jimmy raced to the barn to fetch the nag.
He jumped on her back where the dip made a sag.
"Giddy-up," he urged as he slapped by her tail.
"This is no time to be slow as a snail."
The nag gave it her all, racing the sun.
Jimmy was laughing and having great fun.
When he spied the town through dimming twilight,
He cheered on the mare to continue her flight.
Jimmy was licking and smacking his lips,
Gripping the money pouch around his hips.
He jumped off the nag, and raced into the store.
The shelves were lined with jam jars galore.
He slapped down the coins; bought all in site.
Then thanked the store clerk to be polite.

He opened three jars and sucked them clean.
But he didn't want to seem at all mean.
He opened three more for the nag to slurp.
And the pair moseyed home, having burp
after burp.

"That is nearly the most ridiculous poem I have ever read," King Asterman declared.

"Like I said, I used my good imagination, sir, and I think the rhyming is pretty good. I mean, it's my first very long poem, and I may have broken a rule . . ." She tapped her cheek for a moment. "Come to think of it, some very famous poets have broken the rules about poetry. Although, I think, that's only after they get their famous certificate—"

"Quiet!" King Asterman started squishing and rubbing his face with both hands, making the strangest faces.

Petra tried very hard not to giggle.

Finally, after he had successfully made one hundred different faces, King Asterman said, "Here is your writing certificate." He tossed her a small scroll then clomped to the door. He seemed to have gained his manners back because he flung open the door and pointed the way out.

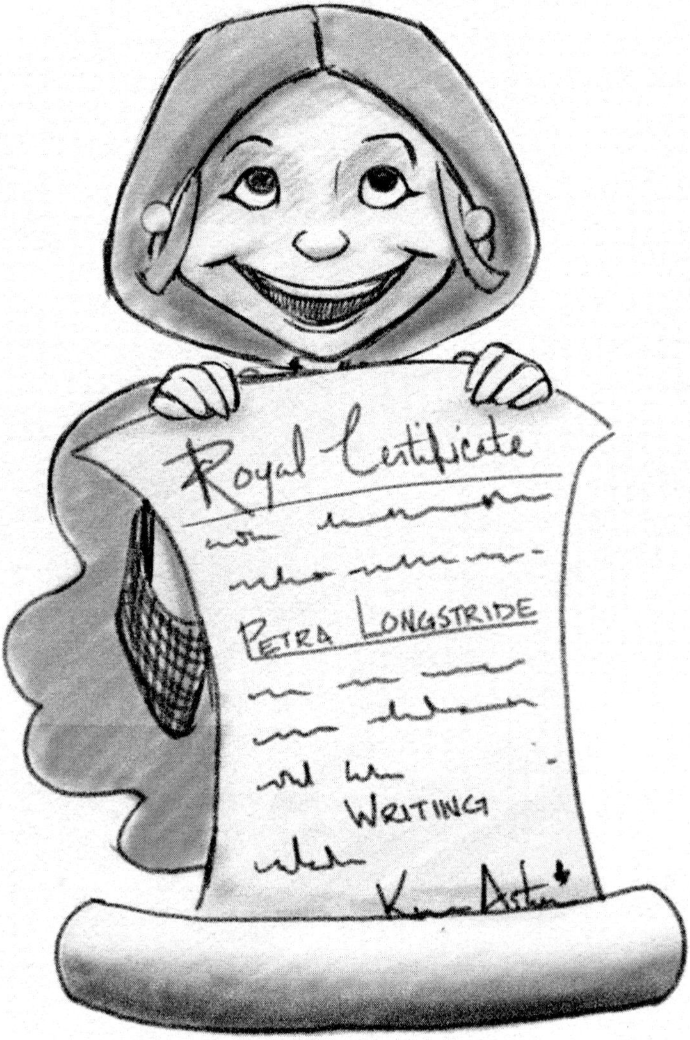
Royal Certificate
Petra Longstride
Writing

Petra raced out of the building, twirling around and waving her certificate in the air. "I did it! I did it! I knew I could if I tried!"

Just then, there was a loud explosion followed by several more, and soon, a few more after that. Snarls was whooping and hollering and scrambling to get all the barbecuers out of Barbeque School as whistling fire flames shot up through the roof and were landing on Crochet School. Duce Crablips peeled out of Crochet School, squealing and twirling while trying to balance a pile of crocheted things on top of his head. The two other crocheters hightailed it behind him.

"Okay, who's to know," Snarls snapped, slapping sparks off his classmates, "that sulfur something-or-other powder is not a seasoning to put on grilled squash!"

King Asterman was charging toward them with outstretched arms and grabbing hands. His face looked very red, maybe even furious.

The three comrades turned and ran. Talent School was definitely over.

CHAPTER 5

THE GANUTES OF THE VAST WILDERNESS

Past the toll bridge and far past the border of the Land of Lost Donkeys, the escaping trio stopped to catch their breath.

"Snarls, were you bumping into me to try to get ahead?" Petra asked, somewhat annoyed.

"No, no. Sorry about that. I just got a little frantic. I don't think I'd like my tail to be cut off and mounted on a slab board."

"Where in the kingdom did you ever get an idea like that?" Petra asked.

"Yuck. How barbaric," Duce whimpered.

"I heard it. That's all." Snarls shuffled his feet. "For instance, in the Kingdom of Boogy Gobees, they cut off a dragon's tail and make trophies to display at the spring equinox celebration. Vicious, vicious creatures they are. Anyway, it gets me all riled up when I'm being chased."

Petra laughed.

Duce gasped.

Snarls hung his head.

"Sorry, Snarls, but that has to be to most ridiculous rumor yet. We'll just have to go there one day to prove you wrong, won't we?"

Snarls looked dizzy. "Go there? Put my life in danger?"

Petra rubbed his nose. "I'll always look out for you, Snarls, just as you look out for me. You know from experience that not all is as it seems, and rumors can't be trusted. And you must admit, you love an adventure as much as I do."

"Well…I guess, yah, that's true," Snarls conceded.

"Shall we head home then and show Father my new certificate and tell him of our new friendship with the Kingdom of Crablips?"

"I can't wait to show my kingdom my new crocheting talent," Duce sighed.

"It's beautiful, Duce. But why is everything pink?" Petra asked.

"Oh, everything in our kingdom is pink. It's just the way of our kingdom. But nobody in my kingdom knows how to crochet. I will be such a hero."

"And I've learned my own valuable cooking lessons," Snarls added.

While heading south, sometimes west, and then sometimes south again, mindlessly leaving the trail to pick fallen nuts, Petra suddenly spotted something poking out from a thick pine tree. Brushing aside the overgrown branches and climbing vines, she discovered a plank of wood with writing on it.

THE VAST WILDERNESS—ENTRÉE AT YOR
OWN RISKY TEMPTACHON
OR BITTER YET
JIST GETT OUT AND KEEP GOING!!

Signed: The Ganutes

"Wow. How did we get so close to the boarder of the Vast Wilderness?" Petra exclaimed.

"Look, not everything that happens is my fault!" Snarls snapped.

"No one is at fault, Snarls. We all weren't paying attention. But this is great! No soldier or adventurer has ever gone into the Vast Wilderness. We should explore! This will make us all heroes in the Kingdom of Pen Pieyu!"

Snarls crossed his front paws. "No way! Not going! It says risky something or other."

"What do you mean? Why hasn't anybody gone there? Why is it called—what's a ganute?" Duce prattled off his questions and gave a good shiver.

"Ganutes are vicious, hideous creatures, all furry and matted, and teeth the size of… of… teeth that can gnaw off a dragon's paw in two bites." Snarls raised his head and snorted out a fire stream.

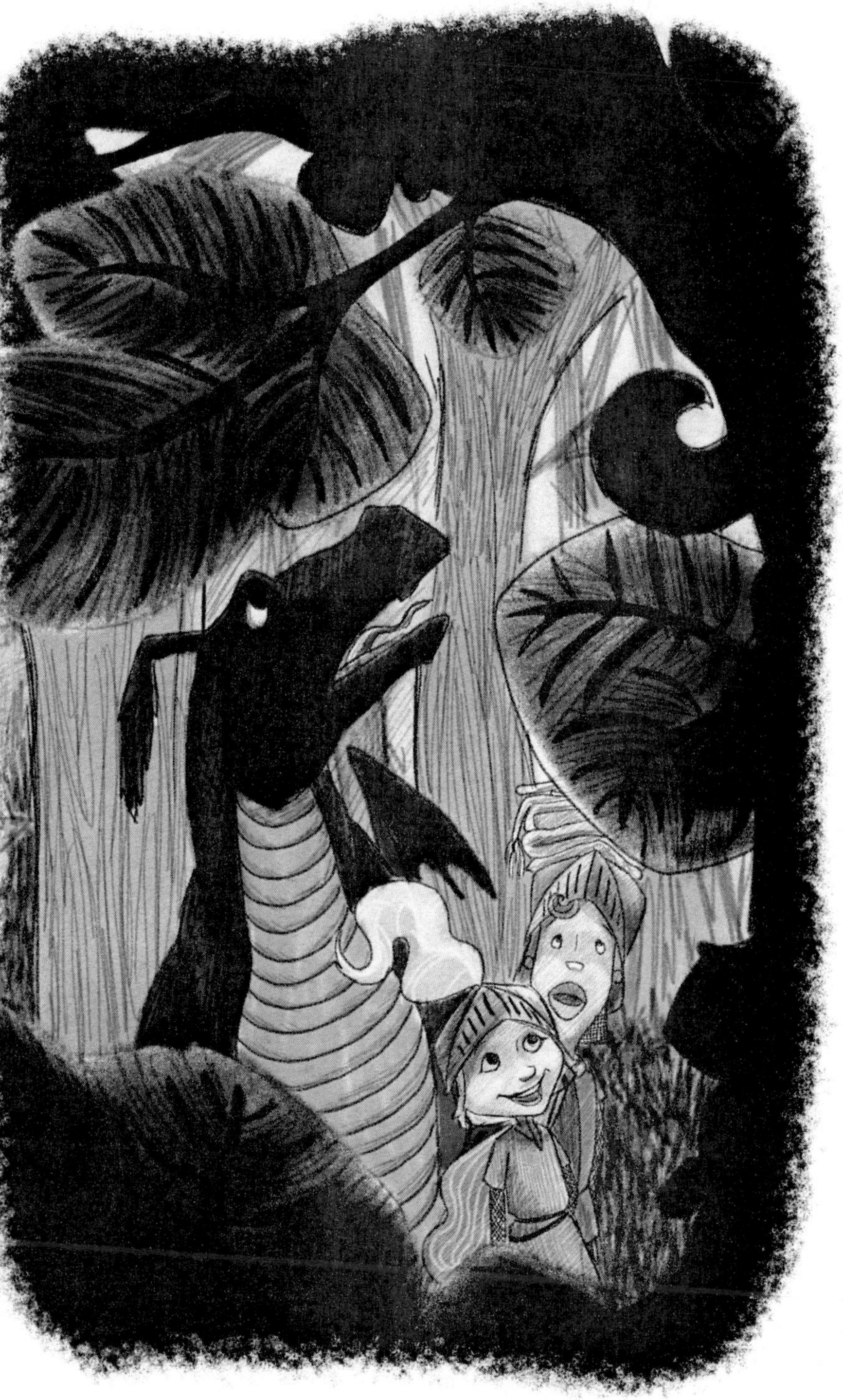

Petra and Duce quickly stomped the sparks that landed on the tall grass all around them.

"Sorry about that. It's just nerves," Snarls apologized; his face reddened.

Petra shook off her own shiver. "That's silly, Snarls. Nobody knows what a ganute is. I say this is the perfect opportunity to explore. We're here. We're going in." Petra raised her cake knife sword and gave the order, "Onward soldiers!"

Snarls moaned, rolled his eyes, then yanked her backwards. "I'll go first, then."

The Vast Wilderness was a dense and dark pine forest with trees taller than any giant Petra had ever seen. Actually, she had never seen a giant, but her good imagination knew precisely how big giants were. Strange shadows seemed to dash out and, then just as quickly, retreat behind the trees as soon as she glanced that way. She tried to tell herself it was just her eyes playing tricks on her, but a tingle crept up her spine just the same. There was no foot path, so Snarls pushed his body through the trees, snapping branches and tossing brush and stumps aside to break the trail ahead of them. Duce was plastered unto Petra's back.

Suddenly, piercing yelping voices broke out all around them. Petra spun around, trying to find where the noise was coming from. She couldn't see anyone. Hard round things started hitting them from every direction. Then, something furry latched on to Petra's face and blinded her eyes.

Petra could hear Snarls and Duce yelling and thrashing about in their own fight. She tried not to scream. "Ahh!" She screamed anyway. "Get off me!" Petra swung her arms, trying to fight off whatever monster it was. She couldn't feel anything around her. Grabbing at the fur over her eyes, she realized it was something small. The something small bit her nose. She flung it off.

"That was just nasty!" she yelled, trying to blink her eyes clear while groping around for her sword. She couldn't find it. She grabbed two onions from her sack, ready to fire them. Whirling around, searching, she finally spotted the culprit on the ground. He was small, small as a royal cucumber. Petra held her onions high, ready to wallop him, if need be. "Get those furballs off my friends! Right now!"

The furry creature, covered with leaves and sticks and dirt, stood up on his hind paws, tilted his chin up, put a front paw into his mouth, and let loose a sharp three-blast whistle. All the other meddling, furry tribe instantly jumped off Snarls and Duce and scurried to form lines behind the whistle blower.

Snarls and Duce scrambled over to stand on either side of Petra.

The whistle-blowing, furry creature puffed up his fur by shaking, then cleared his throat. "My name is Seymour Forest, leader of the ganutes of the Vast Wilderness. And who are you? Can't you read? The sign says, 'No Uninvited Chaos Allowed', or something like that. Besides, we have no donkeys." Seymour started frantically flapping his paws behind his back. "The sign says that too. Well, maybe it's not updated yet. What do you want?"

Just then, Petra spied a bunch of wide-eyed donkeys peeking out from amongst the trees behind Seymour.

She relaxed her onion-throwing arms. "It's okay, really. I'm glad the donkeys are here. I don't blame them for running away. We have just come from Talent School ourselves."

The donkeys glanced around and slowly came forward.

"And we're not here for any chaos. Excuse me, let me introduce ourselves. I am Petra Longstride of the Kingdom of Pen Pieyu and these are my friends, Prince Duce Crablips of the Kingdom of Crablips, and Snarls of the Forest of Doom. We are adventurers."

All the furry creatures started making a fast and excited chit-chit-chit noise. Their leader tried to hush them with another whistle, but that didn't stop their bushy tails from wagging and their "Ooooh"s and "Aaaah"s as they inched their way closer to Petra.

Seymour Forest gave one more shrill, ear-tingling blast. Now the furry tribe had a good silence and froze in their places. "Begging your pardon, Sir Princess Knight. We had no idea it was you," Seymour said, giving a good impression of a royal bow. "And I think you lost this." He struggled to pick up her sword that was twice his size.

Petra slid her sword into her belt and gave a big sigh. Snarls gave a bigger sigh. Duce stood as stiff as a statue with one hand on top of his crochet pile that somehow had remained neatly on top of his head throughout all the chaos.

"How in all the kingdoms do you know I am the Princess Knight?"

"Why, from Bograt, of course," Seymour replied.

"You know Bograt?" Petra, Snarls, and Duce asked in unison.

"And Bograt has been here?" Petra marveled.

"Oh, Bograt, the dear, she brings us onions from time to time—" Seymour clapped a paw over his mouth.

"Onions, hmm. No wonder she wants to take so many home." Petra chuckled, returning the onions she held to her sack.

Seymour blushed. "Really, you don't have to put those away. I mean, we can't grow onions here, and…well, they would be appreciated by the cooks."

Before Petra could hand the onions over properly, two ganutes in white aprons and floppy white hats scurried up her arms, snatched the onions from her hands, and dashed away. The rest of the ganutes dashed in different directions.

"Wait for me!" Snarls hollered and skedaddled after the cooks. "I have the best onion recipes!"

"I'm still surprised that you know Bograt," Petra commented to Seymour. "I didn't know she traveled so far."

"Oh, yes, Bograt was our first foreign visitor. And now, she is a welcome ally in our lands. Of course, that was after we made a pact with her. We give her all the pine nuts she can carry and she doesn't eat us. The deal works out quite nicely." Seymour eyed the ground and kicked up some dirt. "Um, by the way, we won't have to wear frilly dresses, will we? You know, for messing with a knight and missions and all that stuff."

"I don't think so," Petra answered with a light-hearted laugh.

Seymour indicated for her and Duce to follow in the direction the cooks and Snarls had just gone. "Let's get some nut oil on your nose, and here on Prince Duce's ear where he was bit. Sorry about that." He shrugged.

Petra followed Seymour, and Duce followed Petra, and the donkeys, with very big donkey grins, swished their tails and followed everybody.

CHAPTER 6

HOW TO BECOME A ROYAL KNIGHT

After a fabulous supper of roasted onions and pine nuts, onion soup laced with sweet grass, sautéed onions in a hazelnut syrup, and rosehip-fused pine nut stew (all of which Snarls boasted he helped to prepare), they all sat around the fire to relax. The donkeys were just off to the side, munching on hay and pickled onions for dessert.

"You know," Petra said while still pondering the idea, "according to the royal rule book, there are three deeds to choose from to become a royal knight: skinning a crocodile to make his skin into a royal leather chair; eating a roomful of raw onions; or the most recent one added, being the first adventurer to venture into an un-adventured land away from their own land. Father had to take out the deed about hushing the howling dragon, Snarls, since I already did that." Petra winked at Snarls.

"Really, those are the choices?" Duce asked, somewhat distracted since he was teaching some of the ganutes how to crochet.

"Yes. But the best part is that since Bograt is the first adventurer to venture into the lands of the Vast Wilderness, well, quite simply, she is now a royal adventurer," Petra explained.

"Wow!" Seymour gushed, wagging his tail with great speed.

Snarls clicked his claws together. "Does that mean… You're not kidding me now, are you? Bograt will become a knight?"

"Yes, yes. Isn't it wonderful? I will have a fellow knight to train with and do all the knightly things us knights do." Petra smiled. "Although, Bograt has been very busy trying to eat a roomful of raw onions, and I have no doubt she would have finally accomplished that deed, but now, she will be a knight that much sooner."

"Ha ha ha ha ha ha!" Snarls clutched his belly. "Ha ha ha ha! Your father is going to flip his royal crown, and your mother will definitely faint for a week. You have a writing certificate, which is not what the king is expecting at all. Bograt will become a knight. Our new friend is a crochet hero in the Kingdom of Crablips and you don't have to engage him—haha—that's a good pun!" He let go a snort. "Then there's the fact that we have discovered where the lost donkeys are, and we will never, ever tell. Ha ha ha! This is all so hilarious!"

Petra, Duce, and the ganutes all joined in the laughter. The donkeys raised their upper lips in a silent laugh.

"You just never know what's going to happen on an adventure, do you?" Petra bubbled.

Seymour Forest sprang up straight and serious. "You mean anyone of us could become a royal knight if we accomplish one of the deeds?"

All of the ganutes stopped what they were doing and beamed at Petra.

"Of course," Petra answered.

CHAPTER 7

THE ANNOUNCEMENT

The king and queen of Pen Pieyu sat upon their ragged, leather thrones. The queen seemed very stiff, but her bulging eyes darted back and forth. The king's lips were moving, but no words came out. The ganutes were wildly chattering about how any one of them could eat a roomful of raw onions. One ganute bragged that he could definitely tackle the crocodile-skinning event while another asked what a crocodile was. Petra frowned her eyebrows at those two, and the pair went back to chattering about the onion room. The queen yanked off her crown, handed it to the king, and leaned sideways. She looked like she might be relaxing.

"Father, Mother, I have an announcement." Petra peeked into the royal onion room and motioned Bograt to come join her.

"Bograt is our newest knight!" Petra declared.

The royal councilman started turning in circles faster and faster until his robes flew around him with such a flurry that he looked like a Whirling Dervish out of control.

"Stop that!" The king bellowed at him. "Get the royal rule book. Now!" Her father's face turned a painful red color, the same red color that King Asterman could make.

The queen moaned. Petra wondered if she was ill.

The royal councilman dizzily crashed into the ganutes, who crashed into the magician, who crashed into Claymore and rolled him over. There lay the royal rule book, opened and a little crumpled. The councilman smoothed the pages and quickly tossed the book at the king's feet before backing away.

"Father, I can explain," Petra interrupted the commotion. "First of all, these are my new friends, Seymour Forest and the ganutes, from the Land of the Vast Wilderness." She gestured toward the furry creatures now standing in rows and saluting. "They have confirmed that Bograt was the first adventurer to venture into their lands, which, as you know, is one of the deeds in the rule book to become a knight. Therefore, Bograt is a heroine and has earned her knighthood."

Bograt blinked in slow motion for nearly a full minute, then started hopping from one foot to the other. "Oh goody, goody, glee, goody!"

Petra smiled her eyes at her.

"And another piece of very good news for you, Father. I have earned my writing certificate, which makes me the new official storyteller in the Kingdom of Pen Pieyu. We haven't had an

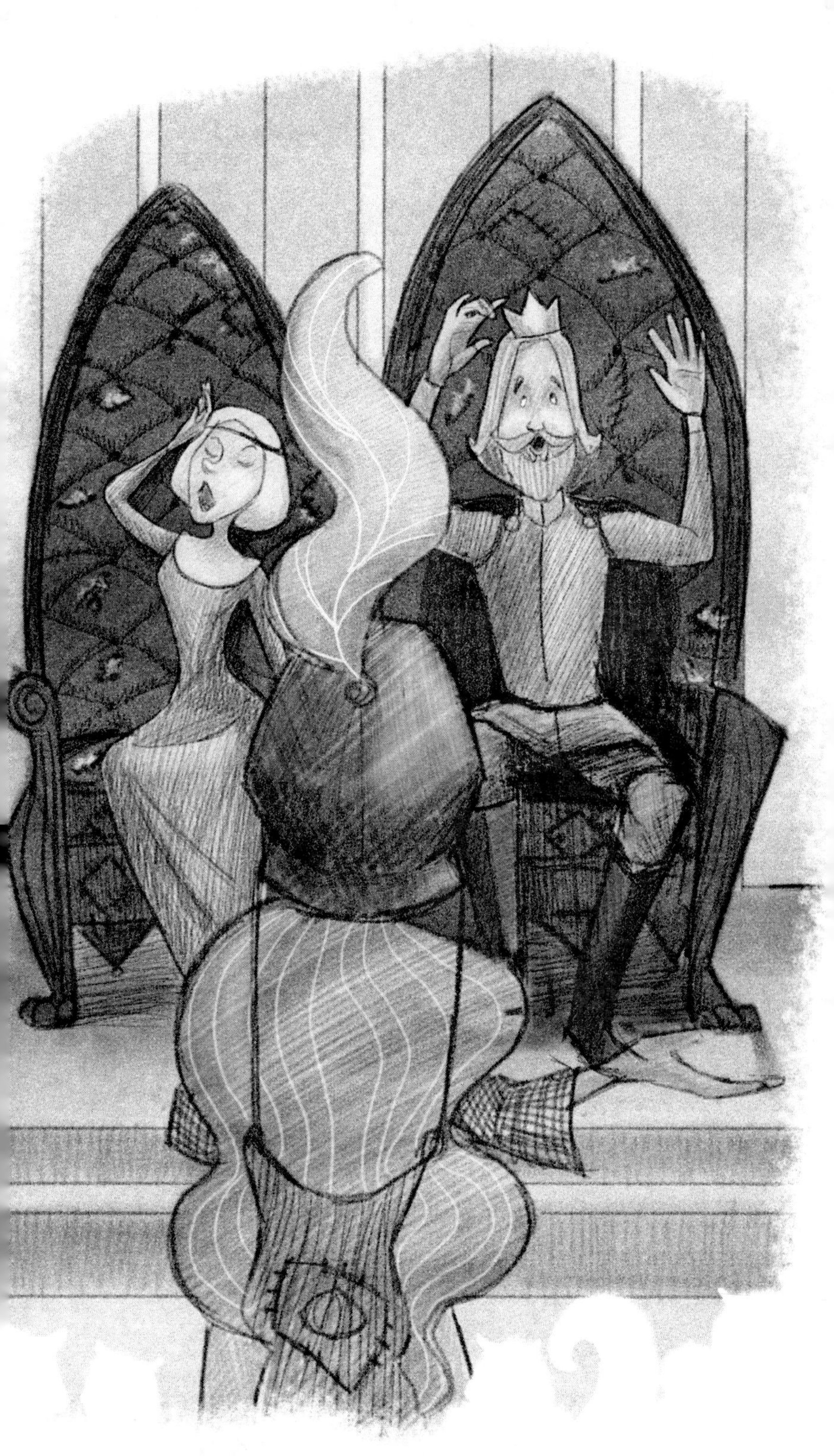

official storyteller since Nana Longstride went off to the West Seas to become an adventurer fifty-nine new moons ago."

"Writing cert—" The king seemed to be stretching up his hair. "How...could ..."

"And who, pray tell, is the pink guy with all the crochet, patting my hand?" the queen muttered.

"Well, this is Prince Duce Crablips. And you both should know all about him since his father sent a scroll introducing him as my soon-to-be fiancé. Father, you really must talk to me more about these things." Petra put her hands on her hips. "Thankfully, we're straightened all that out. Oh, and by the way, the ganutes are going to attempt the deed of eating a roomful of raw onion and become knights themselves."

That moment, the queen fainted. The next moment, the king started groaning, a lot.

"It is all legal, sir." The royal councilman now had the king's scepter in hand, which allowed him to stand quite far back to flip the page and point to a different section in the book. "That particular rule states that anybody that is an invited guest to the Kingdom of Pen Pieyu, and may be invited by anyone that lives in the Kingdom of Pen Pieyu, may access the rules to become a knight of the Kingdom of Pen Pieyu.

And the rule about a venturing adventurer becoming a knight is there also. Look for yourself—you wrote it." The councilman turned and ran.

The king slowly slumped over and looked like he was deflating. After some incoherent mumble-jumble, he wearily raised his arms up into the air. This gesture Petra had seen him do before, and it meant, "You are positively right, my dear."

Petra turned to announce the good news to her friends, but they were already rushing off in different directions. Bograt scurried toward the armoury, the ganutes were running over each other in their race toward the royal onion room, Snarls was headed for the kitchen. Only Duce stayed behind, trying to console the queen with gentle talk of crocheting techniques.

Petra sighed. All was well in the Kingdom of Pen Pieyu.

CHAPTER 8

SIR BOG WITCH BOGRAT

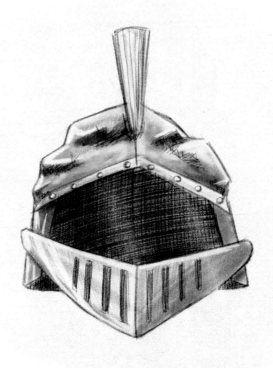

The torch lights were lit, and the band was already playing when the puny Prince Nastybun and his puny knights were announced into the throne room. Their lands to the east, the Kingdom of Mesoggie, was very swampy and damp, and Petra had invited them to come to Pen Pieyu Kingdom whenever they needed to get dry. This, of course, was after Petra and Norton Nastybun had become fast friends, and the knights of Mesoggie were no longer enemies of her kingdom. Prince Nastybun and the puny army were more than excited to learn that Bograt was becoming a knight.

Petra chatted and giggled with Norton as she surveyed the party crowd. The puny army was rolling around beside and on top of Claymore, while the massive dog seemed careful not to squish them. The royal councilman was reading the royal rule book, from a distance, to the king. Duce was humming, crocheting beside the very quiet and still queen. The royal magician was taking bets, from the junior kitchen staff, on a frog race. All nine of the royal palace soldiers showed up as themselves and not frogs, which Petra was very happy about. The ganutes were in the royal onion room, laughing and letting out tremendous burps. Snarls, wearing a white chef's hat and a ruffled apron, had just entered the room juggling six shiny, silver trays of hors d'oeuvres.

That's when the trumpets blared. All heads turned toward the main entrance, toward Bograt. The bog witch beamed and caressed her new armour: her breastplate was rusty and had a crescent moon cut out over her heart, the chain mail leggings had holes cut out in the knees, and the helmet was misshapen and dented as if to fit exactly over the lumps and bumps of her matted and frazzled hair. She looks perfect, Petra thought.

Everybody cheered and whistled, except the king and queen.

Petra motioned the royal magician closer, but she still had to yell over the noise of the rejoicing crowd. "Are you sure you didn't accidently put a spell on my parents? They seem rather, well, frozen."

The royal magician shook his head and yelled back, "No, I did not. They are just stunned. They will get over it eventually."

Bograt came before the king and kneeled. Nothing happened. The crowd started whispering and getting bored. Snarls took charge. He scrambled over to the king, took up the king's

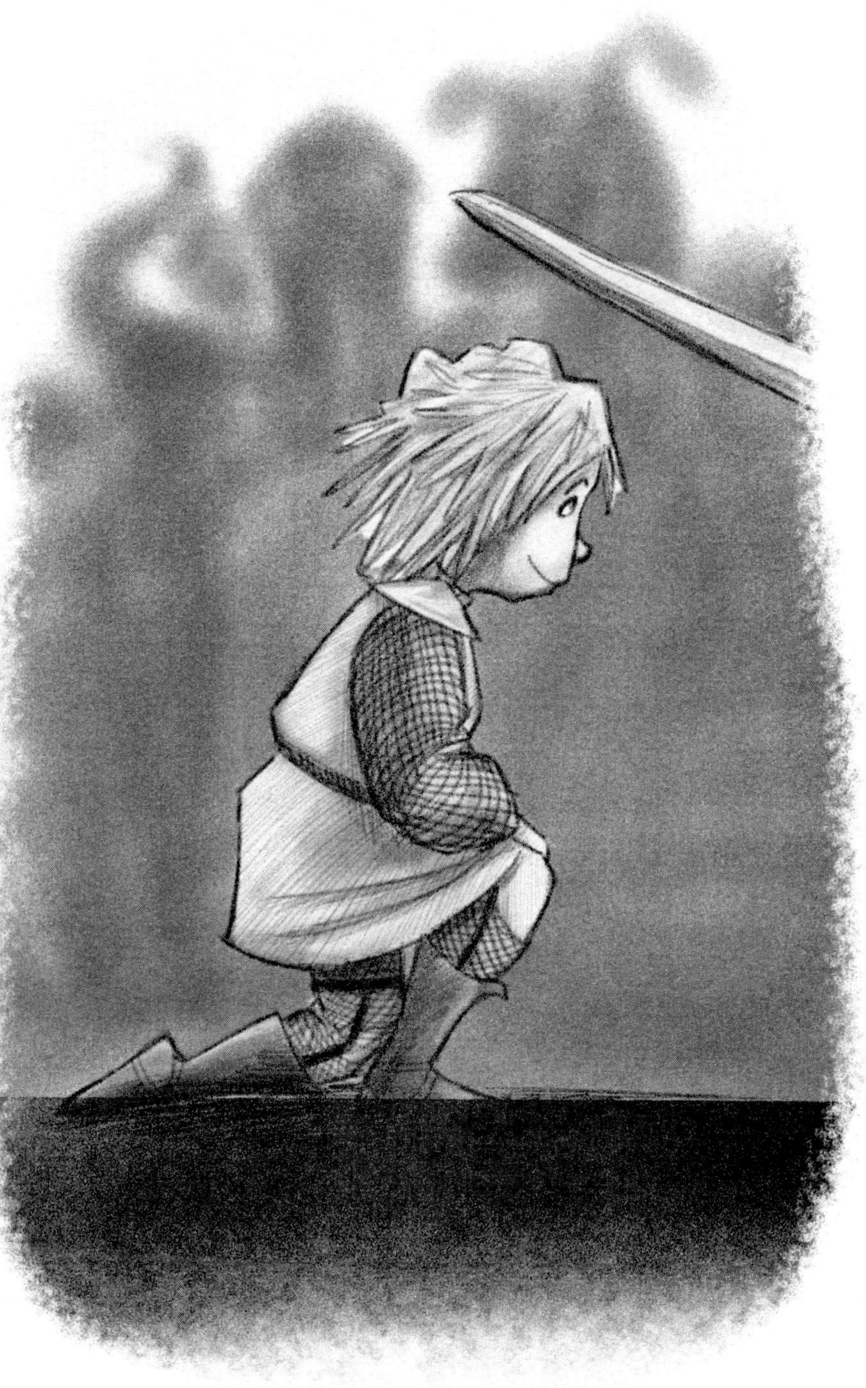

right hand and shook it, as if to make sure it worked, then placed the king's sword in the king's hand and nudged him—twice. The King sighed, re-inflated himself, and lifted his shaking sword to touch Bograt's right shoulder three times. Sounding weary, he said, "I pronounce you Sir Bog Witch Bograt of Kingdom Pen Pieyu."

Bograt turned to face the crowd and show a wide smile of pointy teeth. Everybody cheered, whistled, and threw food at her. The ceremony was complete—this particular food-throwing act completed the knighting ceremony that was reserved for non-family members of the kingdom, according to the royal councilman who read it from the royal rule book

Snarls stepped forward and let out a howl that went on for some time and made everybody's onion juice dance in their glass. The crowd stopped their food-throwing, chattering, cheering, whistling, and in general, all their revelry.

"Hey, everybody! Listen up," Snarls announced. "In honor of Bograt's knighthood, I vote that Petra, the official storyteller of the Kingdom of Pen Pieyu, who has just recently acquired her writing certificate, tell us a story."

A good silence fell over the crowd for quite a long spell. Then some mutterings and mumblings broke out.

"What is a story?" somebody finally asked.

"It's a thing… well… a thing of words," a royal soldier stammered out.

"A thing with lots of words. Scary words!" Seymour Forest squealed. All the ganutes gasped and covered their eyes. Vibrating whimpers burst out from Duce Crablips. Prince Nastybun and the puny army were cramming into a tangled ball of whiny knights. Snarls blew out a fire stream that made everyone cry out and duck.

"Sorry, sorry," Snarls apologized. "I just got a little… uh, nervous."

Petra put out her hands to quiet the crowd. "A story doesn't always have scary words." She glanced toward Bograt, who she suspected had something to do with that rumor. "Some stories are happy or sad or funny. Stories tell a tale worth remembering. They're creative and interesting. Stories have all kinds of characters doing all kinds of things, and sometimes, they have kings and queens and princesses, witches, dragons, magicians and midget knights, pink knights, and even furry creatures."

The crowd stopped their whimpering, muttering, shaking, crying, gasping, whining, and fire breathing. Even the king and queen seemed to have come back to their senses and appeared to be listening. All eyes focused on Petra. She smiled as she gazed over the crowd. "Stories are a good thing."

In no time, the crowd was going wild with the idea. "Story! Story! Story!" they shouted in unison, raising one arm with each new shout.

So a story it was.

CHAPTER 9

THE STORY

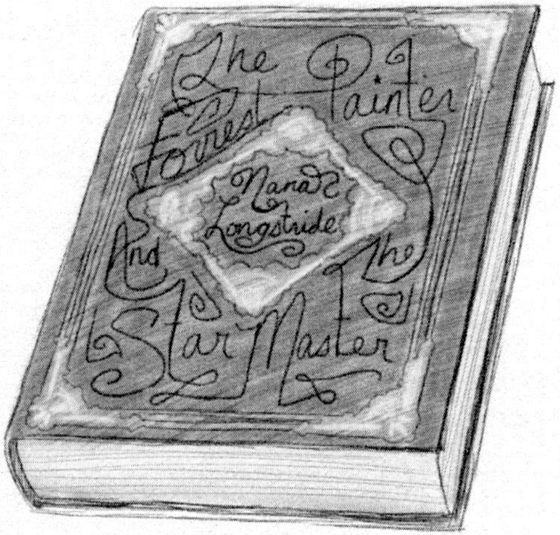
The Forrest Painter
Nana Longstride
And the
Star Master

"I'm going to tell you a story that Nana Longstride wrote a long ago. A story she created with her very good imagination. So everyone must be quiet and still and listen carefully," Petra said, looking at Snarls to reinforce the quiet part. She retrieved a leather-bound book from the secret place on the chalice shelf, opened it, and began to read.

THE FOREST PAINTER AND THE STAR MASTER

Deep in the woods of Majestic Forest, the song of the Great Bugle was just being delivered from the misty heights of Peak Mountain. The changing of the seasons had arrived. Leaf-gathering sprites, cloud-shaping elves, and all the wind weavers recognized the summons and were slowly emerging from their sleepy hollows. Soon, every creature of autumn's magic would be hustling about, eager to perform the duties of the season.

All except one of them.

Aura circled the eldest Poplars, eyeing the trees suspiciously as they swayed and seemed to clap their green arms in anticipation. She tugged the paintbrush from the tangles of her hair and threw it to the ground.

"The forest is too big! I don't know how to do this!" Aura shouted toward the sky.

"But, my lady, you must do it. You are the forest painter now," the pixie, Kepa, spoke softly as she fluttered down to perch on Aura's shoulder. "And by the laws of Majestic Forest, the leaves must breathe with autumn beauty before the frost queen arrives, or she will claim the forest white forever. Look here—the glitters and sparkles and velvet colors. I have them all ready."

Aura flapped her wings hard, sending Kepa tumbling through the air. "My grandmother was the master painter, not me! Then suddenly, she is called upon to paint the heavens where my parents have dwelled forever. I never had time to learn the art. I thought we would have more time together."

Kepa zipped back. "My lady, then might you ask Boreal for help? The star master is a great artist. The elves say he taught them wonderful new images for their cloud art and surely—"

"No, not Boreal! He will try to steal the golden paintbrush from me just as I saw him steal it from my grandmother once."

Kepa placed the golden paintbrush in Aura's palm. "Then you must try by yourself. But sometimes it is worth knowing that you must see with your heart, not only your eyes."

Aura stood in silence for some time.

"Get the glitter paint ready," she ordered. "At least, my eyes tell me I have work to do."

Throughout the day, Kepa mixed and toned the paint while Aura hovered above the trees, splashing thick streams of glitter onto the leaves.

"My lady, the sun will soon sleep beyond Peak Mountain, and I fear you have not accomplished as much as need be done."

"I still have time." Aura glanced at the deep hues of pink and purple as dusk settled on the horizon, creating a cape around Peak Mountain. She inhaled a deep breath of the crisp fall air. "Prepare the sparkles, Kepa."

Aura slapped the brush into the new color and flew with spins and dives, splattering sparkle globs over the still wet glitter.

Suddenly, Kepa shrieked out. "I'm sure the frost queen's fingers have, just now, tickled my spine. She is nearer than the north wind has told. Will you not reconsider? I'm sure Boreal would help."

"No. I can do it alone!" Aura snapped, wiping her forehead. But she too had felt the icy breath on the back of her neck, and it taunted her with whispers of its claim to the forest. "Look, the moonlight has come on now. We can work through the night. Hurry yourself. Finish with the velvet paint."

Aura took the whole bucket of velvet paint and, flying in a zigzag pattern, tilted the pail enough to let the paint spill out in a steady stream. She returned for the second bucket just as clouds started dancing across the moon. The shadows made it difficult for her to tell where she had left off. An idea sprung to her. In one swift motion, she heaved the full bucket up and flung the velvet paint into the night.

A weary excitement came over her as she caught glimpses of the velvet curtain slithering over the leaves and down the tree trunks.

"See, Kepa, I'm nearly half done and it is not even nearing the dawn."

"Yes, my lady," the pixie whispered, "but is the soul of autumn here?"

Aura fluttered down to the ground and wrapped her wings tightly around her body. She shivered as she listened to the "thup, thup, thup" of the paint dripping off the leaves like tears.

"You are right," Aura finally decided. "My grandmother's pride is not here. Even the call of

the loon is sadder than usual, as if they too feel the sorrow of this autumn."

Aura stood up tall. "Call for the star master, Kepa. I need help. Majestic Forest must not be lost to the frost queen's icy touch!"

Guided by a wind weaver, Kepa soared off on the wings of the wind, soon to return with Boreal to the forest.

~~~~~~~~~~~~~~~~~

"Why, Aura," came a thundering voice from above, "what artist has created autumn this year?" He pushed back the hood of his cloak, revealing his wrinkled face, and long hair and beard that fell in tangled knots.

Aura clenched her fists. "Boreal, I need help. I fear the frost queen's arrival by this moondown. My heart is willing to forgive you if you will help me save the autumn."

"Forgive me?" Boreal's laughter sent the clouds scattering. "My dear child, I have done you no wrong. My life is in the night sky, creating images of heroes and beasts in the stars and painting the faces of the moon that forever watch over Majestic Forest."

"Then why did you steal the golden paintbrush from my grandmother?" Aura demanded. "I recognized your cloaked figure when you took it from the edge of the river one night."

Boreal smiled and gently touched her wing. Aura felt an energy, like a burst of warm tingles rush through her. "I was only returning the brush to a forgetful old lady," Boreal assured her. "You can trust in me, as well as you should trust in yourself."

Aura stared into the star master's ancient face. She noticed how his green eyes twinkled with the same kindness as her grandmother's. He suddenly seemed very wise.

"Boreal, will you show me? We haven't much time."

"To be a great artist, you must create with passion," Boreal instructed eagerly. He clasped Aura's hand in his and, with a light, sweeping motion, guided her to gently brush the leaves with a caress of paint. Her tender touch made the paint spread easily, and the trees seemed to bow down, allowing the leaves to reach out to her. While practicing this new art, she also discovered that a different combination of the colors created a more desired effect. Before long, she was gliding gracefully, as if to some unheard music, spreading ribbons of billowing velvet and glitter paint behind her.

A sudden rage of icy balls plummeted from the sky. Aura fumbled the brush, nearly losing it to the river below. Gripping the brush tighter, she frantically beat her wings against the stinging balls and shot up over the treetops.

"Boreal, Kepa, I must finish the canopy," she called down to them. "I need help. Get the sparkles to me, spread them high and wide. Please hurry!"

Kepa hastily stirred the sparkles to bubble up in the last buckets of paint and placed them inside Boreal's cloak. With a swift and precise sweep of his arm, he raised his cloak to cover all the forest and the sky as he flung the sparkles up toward Aura.

Aura beat her wings with such force that they ached. She fretted over how she could possibly catch all of the sparkles before they hit the ground. She concentrated on her task harder. Her concentration seemed to make the icy balls slow and not sting as hard, while the sparkles seemed to just hover in the air as if waiting for her. It felt as if time was nearly standing still and as if the whole forest had become one with her in her effort to create the autumn.

She gasped when she realized that this power, this magic, was within herself—she just had to believe to realize. Quickly, she took a deep breath, spread her wings wide, and willingly fell into the waltzing dance of the wind. The mystical rhythm of her new flight allowed her to soar with masterful elegance and timeless speed, to precisely zip between every icy ball, and to easily gather the sparkles and offer each leaf its sparkle crown.

At the same moment that her paintbrush kissed the last leaf, Boreal's cloak fell back, taking the icy balls and clouds away in its folds. There was a trail of fading light behind the moon as if it had just swung back into its position to smile upon the forest again.

Autumn twinkled like a stash of jewels.

Kepa cheered.

Boreal nodded and smiled.

Then, the finale of Aura's thoughts performed—the glitter and sparkles and velvet colors swirled into a whirlwind that shot upward, bursting into an explosion of lights that danced across the night sky.

Aura's heart swelled with a pride she never felt before as she gazed over her masterpiece of autumn. And just for a breath, as a happy tear rolled down her cheek, she thought she saw her grandmother smiling down at her from the heavens.

EPILOGUE

There were some sniffling noises and one loud nose-blowing noise, but besides that, you could have heard a pin drop in the royal throne room. Snarls had a dreamy look as he passed a claw under his eye. Bograt was hugging a surprised-looking Prince Nastybun. The puny army was cuddled up with the ganutes to form a mass of knights and fur. The royal councilman and the royal magician were holding hands with the royal soldiers. Duce had crawled up onto the queen's lap and she had her arm around him.

Petra wiped away her own tear—a tear of happiness and pride. Pride that the story she told had left an impression on her listeners. Happiness that the king and queen were beaming at her with admiration. Happiness that stories would be back in the Kingdom of Pen Pieyu. And pride in knowing that she too, with much practice and using her good imagination, would one day write great stories, just like Nana Longstride.

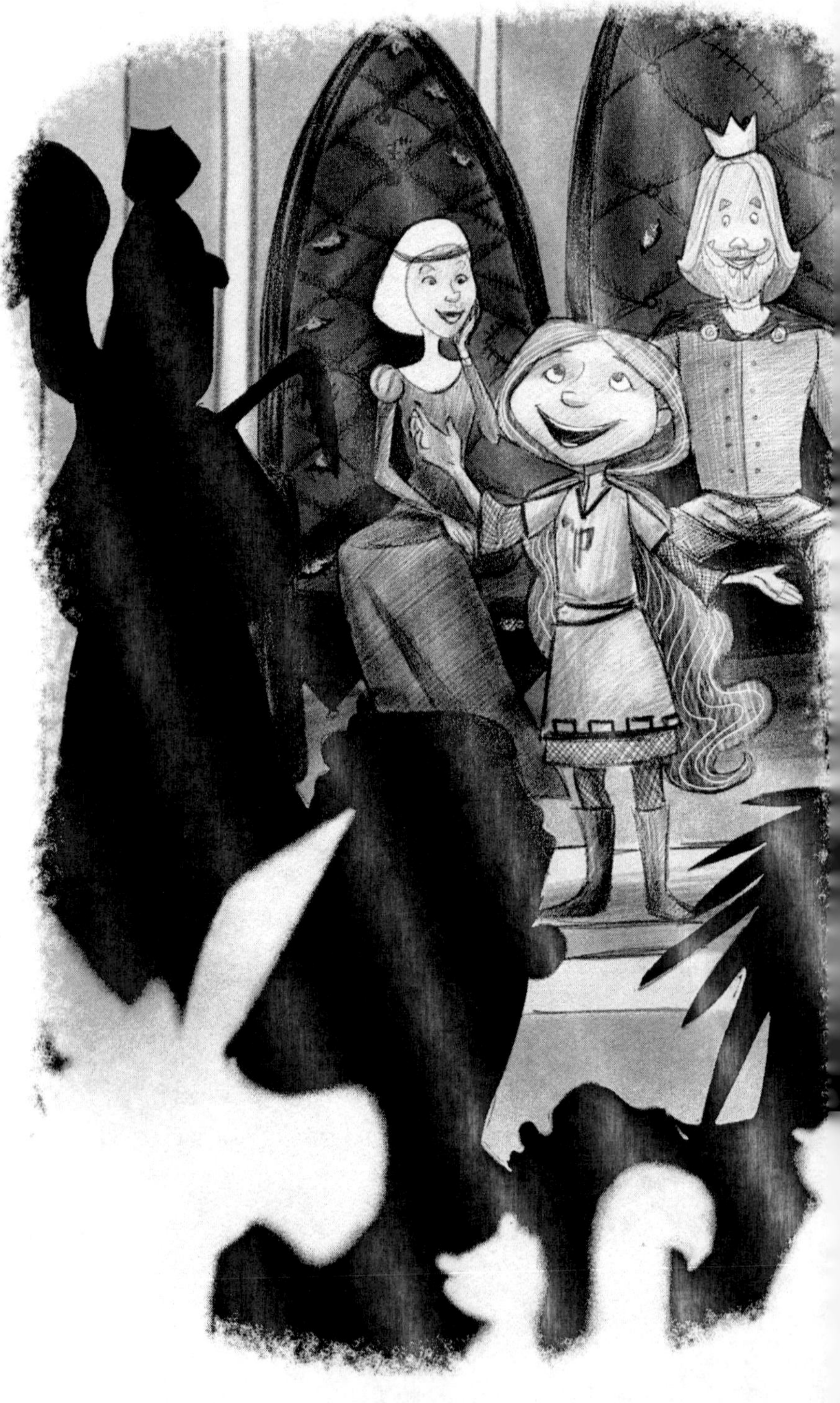

Sir Princess Petra's Talent is a
multi-award winning book.

Author's website: www.dragonsbook.com